♥

This igloo book belongs to:

....

igloobooks

Published in 2013
by Igloo Books Ltd
Cottage Farm
Sywell
NN6 0BJ
www.igloobooks.com

Text and illustrations © 2009 Humphrey's Corner Limited

Humphrey's Corner

Sally Hunter

www.humphreys-corner.com

Adapted from Humphrey's Playtime
First published in 2001 by The Penguin Group

FIR003 0513
2 4 6 8 10 9 7 5 3
ISBN: 978-1-78197-301-1

Printed and manufactured in China

Humphrey's Playtime

Sally Hunter

Humphrey doesn't go to school yet,
so he has lots of time to play.

He gets everything out of his box...

... the train, blocks, boat, octopus,
caterpillar... and all the other toys.

other days, Humphrey plays with his
special painted animals. "All aboard!" he says.
"We are going on an adventure."

"Come on, Pinky, up you go."

And sometimes Humphrey paints a lovely picture for Mum.
She especially likes rainbows and smiley sunshine faces.

"Da da da daaaa...
I'm a Superhero!"
shouts Humphrey.

He runs around
the house, jumps off
the chairs and makes
a lot of noise!

"Have you finished saving the world yet?"
asks Mum.

Humphrey likes playing
dress-up in big shoes!

He walks about in them.
Clomp, Clomp!

Dad was late for work because his
best shoes were in the toy box.
oh, Humphrey!

Henry Horse takes Humphrey on long journeys
to different lands. It is very exciting!

But they have to be back in time for tea.

one time, Humphrey got lost at sea...
there were lots of monsters!
Good job mop came to help.

Humphrey has lots of fun in the garden, too.
He has a look for George, who lives next door.

Then makes roads for his cars and trucks...

... and builds little houses out of stones for the fairies.

In the garden, Humphrey has his very own swing.

"Hello Miss Birdy. How are you today?" he asks.

Humphrey has some creepy crawly friends, too.
"Come on, Simon, Sally and Sam Snail," he says.
"off we go! Choo, Choo!"

Dad gets Humphrey's bike out of the garage.
"Look, Dad! Soon I can go on a big boy's bike!"

"Come on, Mop, we are going for a ride.
Hold on tight!"

Humphrey has lots of lovely days,
playing in all these different ways...

But most of all,
Humphrey likes...

... looking after...

... cuddling...

SH

... playing with...

... and loving mop- his soft,
floppy, one-eared little rabbit. x

Goodbye, Humphrey.
See you soon!